PREHISTORIC
OCEANS

PREHISTORIC OCEANS

AN EXPLORER'S GUIDE

BY WARREN ALLMON, PH.D.

OF THE PALEONTOLOGICAL RESEARCH INSTITUTION

RUNNING PRESS
PHILADELPHIA · LONDON

Copyright © 1996 by Running Press

Printed in Canada

All rights reserved under the Pan-American and International Copyright Conventions.
This book may not be reproduced in whole or in part in any form or by any means, electronic or mechanical, including photocopying, recording, or by any information storage and retrieval system now known or hereafter invented, without written permission from the publisher.

9   8   7   6   5   4   3   2   1
Digit on the right indicates the number of this printing.

Library of Congress Cataloging-in-Publication
  Number 94–73895
ISBN 1–56138–593–X

Cover and interior design by Linda Chiu Barber
  and Paul Kepple
Picture research by Susan Oyama
Edited by Brian Perrin
The text was set in Galliard and Caslon Antique

Package front and back cover illustrations by Bob Walters. Copyright © 1996 by Bob Walters. Pacakge back cover photograph courtesy Department of Library Services, American Museum of Natural History (Neg. 336000, photo by J. Beckett). Book cover illustration by Bob Walters. Copyright © 1996 by Bob Walters.

Book interior illustrations:

Courtesy Department of Library Services, American Museum of Natural History: pp. 21 top (Neg. 120811, photo by Thane Bierwert), bottom (Neg. 120810 photo by Thane Bierwert); 24 top (Neg. 124610, photo by Eugene Rota), bottom (Neg. 124607, photo by Eugene Rota); 39 (Neg. 336000, photo by J. Beckett); 62–63 (Neg. 126010).

Andrew H. Knoll, Harvard University: pp. 14–15.

Paleontological Research Institution/Wendy L. Taylor, photographer: pp.19 bottom left, 20, 22 bottom, 23 bottom, 25 top, 33 bottom right, 34, 48–49, 52.

Smithsonian Institution: title page (photo no. 86-2407), pp. 10–11 (photo no. 85–16648), 16–17 (photo no. 86–2407); 25 bottom (photo no. 87–7507); 26–27 (photo no. 90–14564); 58 (photo no. 86–12842).

United States Geological Survey Photographic Library, Denver: pp. 41 top (photo by P.T. Hayes, 53), bottom (photo by R.G. Reeves, 12); 42 (photo by P.B. King, 460); 46–47 (photo by M. Gordon, Jr., 49).

Bob Walters: pp. 22 top, 28–32, 37, 43.
Copyright © 1996 by Bob Walters.

This book may be ordered by mail from the publisher. Please add $2.50 for postage and handling.
But try your bookstore first!
Running Press Book Publishers
125 South Twenty-second Street
Philadelphia, Pennsylvania 19103–4399

CONTENTS

INTRODUCTION

Millions of years ago, sea monsters swam the Earth's oceans. Strange shrimp with fierce biting teeth; 50-foot-long swimming lizards; sea scorpions with huge, grasping claws; and 60-foot-long sharks with enormous jaws are just a few of the terrifying and fascinating creatures that hunted the depths of the prehistoric seas. There were other creatures—not so scary but just as strange—that lived in the oceans: jawless fish, animals with plant-like stalks that made them look like flowers, giant clams that looked like corals, relatives of modern squid that looked like snails.

The world's oceans have undergone enormous changes since these weird and wonderful "monsters" lived in their waters. They've changed location, shape, size, and temperature. The creatures living in them have died out or evolved into new life forms. Mass extinctions have wiped away thousands—perhaps millions—of species that will never swim the Earth's oceans again.

How do we know where ancient oceans were or what kind of animals and plants lived in them? What happened to change the oceans, and what became of the creatures living in them? This book will show you how scientists have investigated these questions. It will answer some of the questions for you, but it will also show you how to find your own answers. So get ready to dive into the fascinating world of prehistoric oceans!

PART ONE

WATER, WATER EVERYWHERE

Our planet, the Earth, is special. It's the only planet we know of in the universe where water is found in liquid form. More than three quarters of the Earth's surface is covered by liquid water, and most of this water is in the oceans.

When the Earth first formed from a spinning cloud of dust and gas around five billion years ago, it was very hot—much hotter than it is today. It had no atmosphere and no oceans.

As the Earth cooled, gases came out of the crust and collected around the planet to form the first atmosphere—a protective envelope of gases that surrounds the Earth. One of these gases was water vapor, or steam. As the Earth continued to cool, the water vapor in the atmosphere condensed, or turned into liquid. This liquid fell to the Earth as rain.

It rained and rained for millions of years. It rained so much that the low places on the Earth's surface filled with water. These were the first oceans. There have been oceans on Earth ever since.

Some planets in our solar system are closer to the sun than the Earth is. These planets are too hot for liquid water. The average surface temperature of Venus—the next planet closer to the sun—is more than 475°C, or 887°F! (The Earth's average surface temperature is about 15°C, or 60°F, and the hottest temperature ever recorded on Earth was 58°C, or 136°F.) Because water boils and turns into steam at 100°C (212°F), there can be no liquid water on Venus, but its atmosphere contains a lot of steam.

Planets that are farther from the sun than the Earth is—such as Mars, the next planet farther away—are too cold to have liquid water. There is evidence (such as valleys that appear to have been carved by flowing water) that there was once liquid water on Mars, but the average surface temperature is –23° C (–10°F) today. Because water freezes into ice at 0° C (32°F), there can be no liquid water on Mars now.

The Earth happens to be just the right distance from the sun to have liquid water. This makes Earth very special, because without liquid water, there could be no life.

THE BEGINNING OF LIFE ON EARTH

Every living thing on Earth is made, in part, of water. And every living thing on Earth needs water to survive. This is because water allows all the chemicals in living things to move around and react with each other. Almost everything living things do, like breathing and digesting and reproducing,

can only happen in water. This is one reason we believe that life on Earth first arose in the water.

The oldest known *fossils*—remains or traces of life from the past preserved in the crust of the Earth—are more than three and a half billion years old. They are very small and are the remains of single cells of organisms like the bacteria that live in water today. These fossils suggest that life on Earth must have begun some time before three and a half billion years ago.

Most scientists believe life began when chemicals in the ocean combined to form molecules like RNA and DNA, which are the basic building blocks of all living things. These molecules combined with others that had also formed in the ocean and made the first living cells. All of this had to have happened before three and a half billion years ago. And it probably happened in the oceans.

GEOLOGICAL TIME SCALE

The Geological Time Scale shown on page 13 is the system of names and dates used by all paleontologists to organize the history of life.

The chart shows the three major eras and the periods of time within each era, as well as some of the organisms that lived on Earth at the same time.

The dates given represent the number of years ago each period began.

ERA	PERIOD	YEARS AGO	SOME LIFE FORMS
CENOZOIC	Recent	11 Thousand	Human beings and other mammals, *Carcharadon megalodon* and other sharks, crabs, starfish, snails, sea urchins
CENOZOIC	Pleistocene	3 Million	
CENOZOIC	Pliocene	13 Million	
CENOZOIC	Miocene	25 Million	
CENOZOIC	Oligocene	36 Million	
CENOZOIC	Eocene	58 Million	
CENOZOIC	Paleocene	65 Million	
MESOZOIC	Cretaceous	135 Million	*Tyrannosaurus rex*, pterodactyls, mosasaurs, plesiosaurs, ichthyosaurs, ammonoids, rudists
MESOZOIC	Jurassic	180 Million	
MESOZOIC	Triassic	240 Million	
PALEOZOIC	Permian	280 Million	*Osteichthyes, Chondrichthyes, Anomalocaris,* trilobites, crinoids
PALEOZOIC	Pennsylvanian	310 Million	
PALEOZOIC	Mississipian	345 Million	
PALEOZOIC	Devonian	405 Million	
PALEOZOIC	Silurian	425 Million	
PALEOZOIC	Ordovician	500 Million	
PALEOZOIC	Cambrian	550 Million	
PRECAMBRIAN TIME			Ediacara organisms

PART TWO

LIFE IN THE OCEANS, PAST AND PRESENT

Humans are mammals. Mammals are similar to other animals—such as reptiles, amphibians, fish, and birds—in one very obvious way. All have a backbone or spine made of a chain of bones called *vertebrae*. Animals with backbones are called *vertebrates*.

Because we are vertebrates, we tend to think that most of the world is like us. But most of the animals in the world are spineless. Most animals in the world, both today and in the past, are *invertebrates*.

The number of different kinds of animals in the ocean has changed over time. When we look at the number of animal species living in ancient oceans, we notice something very quickly. At certain times in the

Fossil *Charnia*,
an *Ediacara organism*,
found in southern Australia.
(More than 550 million years old.)

history of life, many kinds of organisms have disappeared suddenly and never returned.

When all the animals of a particular kind die, that kind is said to have become *extinct*. When many kinds of animals become extinct in a short period of time, we call that a *mass extinction*.

Organisms that survive mass extinctions often change over time, from generation to generation, through a process called *evolution*. Scientists believe this is how new kinds of plants and animals appear on Earth to replace the ones that have become extinct.

There have been five major mass extinctions over the last 600 million years. Each time, thousands of kinds of plants and animals disappeared in a relatively short time (several years to several million years). New plants and animals eventually evolved to take their places, but for a while after each mass extinction, the world probably looked very empty and lonely.

PRECAMBRIAN OCEAN LIFE

Once life arose in the oceans, not much happened for a long time. At least not much that we can see by studying fossils.

The oldest known fossils are microscopic. They are the remains of bacteria preserved in

Fossil *Inkrylovia*, an *Ediacara organism*, found in Russia's White Sea region. (More than 550 million years old.)

15

Ediacara organisms swim in the Precambrian sea.

rocks from Australia that are more than three and a half billion years old.

For most of the first two billion years of life on Earth, living things remained very simple and very small. Then, some time before about 600 million years ago, near the end of what is known as Precambrian time, simple single-celled organisms evolved into more complex multicellular organisms. The oldest fossils of multicellular organisms were first found in the Ediacara Hills of southern Australia, and are known as *Ediacara organisms.*

The Ediacara fossils are very puzzling. Some resemble animals that live in modern oceans. Others are unlike anything alive today. Some scientists think that the Ediacara organisms were an early, failed attempt to build multicellular organisms. Others think that at least some Ediacara organisms survived and evolved into organisms that lived on in ancient oceans.

PALEOZOIC LIFE IN THE OCEANS

About 550 million years ago, at the beginning of the Cambrian Period of the Paleozoic Era, something remarkable happened. In rocks of about this age, we can see the first records of many kinds of multicellular animals. Most scientists believe that this event represents the beginning of most of the basic kinds of animals we see in the world today. This event—the sudden explosion of new, complex life forms—is known as the *Cambrian Explosion.*

The Cambrian Explosion was the start of a new era that lasted from

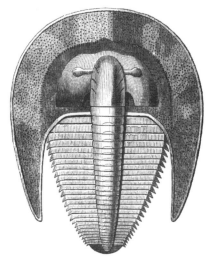

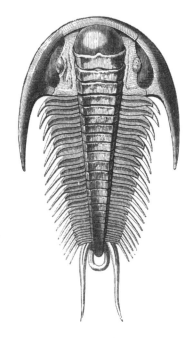

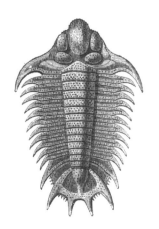

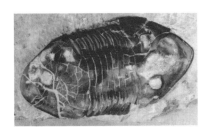

Drawings of trilobites (above)
and a fossil trilobite (left)
found in New York.
Trilobites were common
in Paleozoic oceans.

about 550 to about 240 million years ago. This period of time is known as the Paleozoic ("ancient life") Era. Imagine that you could travel back in time and snorkel in a Paleozoic ocean. (This would be a long trip, because humans did not evolve until almost half a billion years later!) Many of the animals you would see would look strange and unusual, because life in the oceans has changed dramatically over the last 500 million years.

Paleozoic oceans were dominated by different groups of animals than later oceans. One of the most common groups was the *trilobites* (TRY-lo-bites)—distant relatives of modern crabs and lobsters. Trilobites are extinct today, but

Brachiopod fossils.

during the Paleozoic Era they thrived in the seas. Some swam or floated, but most trilobites probably crawled on the bottom and fed on debris.

Another very common group of Paleozoic sea animals was the *brachiopods* (BRAK-ee-o-pahds). A few kinds of brachiopods are still alive today, but they are rare and live in hidden places, such as in caves or under rocks. Brachiopods look like clams, but they are very different inside. Both clams and brachiopods have two hard shells, but brachiopods do not have the clams' large muscular foot that is used to dig into the mud or sand.

Also very common in Paleozoic seas was a group of animals that look

a bit like plants. *Crinoids* (CRIN-oyds), or "sea lilies," looked like starfish on a stalk. They are relatives of the starfish, but their arms faced up into the water instead of down onto the sea floor.

A few kinds of crinoids are alive today, but they are rare and live in cold, deep, and out-of-the-way places. In the Paleozoic Era, they were very abundant. There were so many of them that some rocks from that time are made up of almost nothing but the skeletons of crinoids!

Crinoid fossils (above and bottom right).

There were predators in Paleozoic oceans, too. Some of these were very large, at least by Paleozoic standards.

In the earliest part of the Paleozoic Era, the largest known animal was also the most fearsome predator. It is known as *Anomalocaris* (a-no-ma-lo-KER-is), which means "strange shrimp." It was strange indeed—so strange that we don't really know what group of animals it belonged to.

There is nothing like *Anomalocaris* alive today. It was between three and six feet long, and it had large grasping forelimbs and a circular, multi-toothed mouth. Some trilobites have been found with bite marks in their tails—probably from *Anomalocaris*'s fierce teeth!

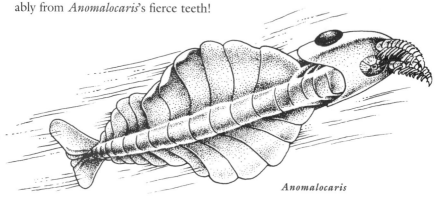

Anomalocaris

Eurypterids (you-RIP-ter-ids), or "sea scorpions," were another group of animals that included some fearsome predators. Now extinct, eurypterids were most closely related to today's horseshoe crabs. They ranged in size from a few inches to seven feet long. The largest ones had huge claws for grasping fish and other prey.

Eurypterid fossil.

Nautiloids (NAW-ti-loyds) are relatives of the modern squid and octopus, but they have a hard shell. There is only one kind of nautiloid living today—the chambered nautilus. During the Paleozoic Era, however, there were many kinds of nautiloids, in many shapes and sizes. The largest was more than 20 feet long! Like

Drawings of nautiloids (above) and a fossil nautiloid (bottom right).

the modern nautilus, Paleozoic nautiloids were probably all predators. They most likely swam and floated in the sea, catching prey in their tentacles and cutting it up with their sharp, parrot-like beaks.

Early multicellular life in the oceans was all

invertebrate, but in rocks around 500 million years old we begin to find the first fossil bones—the oldest known traces of vertebrates.

Agnaths were jawless, armored fish. At right is a plaster model of a Devonian *Agnath* (about 400 million years old). Below is a model of a Silurian *Agnath* (about 420 million years old).

The first vertebrates were fish, but they looked very different from most fish we know today. They had no jaws, and probably fed by sucking mud off the sea floor. Many had thick, bony armor on their backs to protect them from large predators such as the eurypterids.

By around 400 million years ago, some fish had developed jaws. Some jawed fish became fierce predators themselves. One group, which scientists call *Chondrichthyes* (con-DRIK-thee-ees), or "cartilaginous fish," had skeletons made largely of a soft, protein-rich material called cartilage. These were the ancestors to today's sharks and rays. Another group, called *Osteichthyes* (ah-stee-IK-thee-ees), or "bony fish," had skeletons made mostly of hard bone. These were the ancestors of today's salmon, tuna, and many other kinds of fish.

Osteichthyes fossil.

Over the years, some of these bony fish ventured from the sea into fresh-water rivers, streams, and ponds. It was probably there, in fresh waters, that fish-like animals developed the first lungs and legs, and took their first steps out of water onto land. Their descendants are the amphibians, reptiles, birds and mammals—including humans—of today.

The Paleozoic Era ended about 240 million years ago, when the largest mass extinction in the history of life took place. As much as 90 percent of all the different kinds of organisms on Earth may have disappeared over a period of a few million years. (This may sound like a long time, but it really isn't, when you think about how old the Earth is!)

Eusthenopteron,
a fish that crawled on land.

Pictured here is the earliest known amphibian: *Ichthyostega*, a descendant of *Eusthenopteron* (see page 25). Fish like *Eusthenopteron* probably evolved the ability to crawl on land so that they could move from one freshwater pool to another to avoid seasonal droughts. Over millions of years of this forced crawling, these fish evolved even better means of surviving out of water. Some of their descendants, the amphibians, continued the transition to life on land.

We don't know for sure what caused this catastrophe, but most of the evidence suggests that there were several causes. At about this time, all the Earth's continents drifted together to form one huge "supercontinent." The supercontinent had less total shoreline than the separate continents had. Many animals had lived near the shores, and when the shores disappeared, they lost their habitat. The climate also changed and became unlivable for many animals.

Whatever the cause, the oceans looked very different after this mass extinction, because

Elasmosaurus,
a plesiosaur.

many of the animals that had been so common in the Paleozoic seas were gone. In their place arose other, very different animals. The world has never been the same since.

MESOZOIC LIFE IN THE OCEANS

The period of time between 240 million and 65 million years ago is called the Mesozoic ("middle life") Era. You may know it as the Age of

Reptiles, because this was when the dinosaurs ruled the land, and other large reptiles flew through the air.

It was also the era of sea monsters—large marine reptiles that looked like something out of a nightmare.

Mosasaurs (MO-suh-sores) were enormous lizards that swam in the seas that covered what are now places like Kansas, North Carolina, and Germany. Some were more than 50 feet long! *Plesiosaurs* (PLEE-see-o-sores) were long-necked, toothy reptiles that reached similarly enormous sizes.

Icthyosaurs (IK-thee-o-sores) were reptiles shaped like modern porpoises and dolphins, which are mammals. Like dolphins, icthyosaurs swam actively through the ocean. Beautifully preserved fossils

An ichthyosaur.

of icthyosaurs tell us that they had a fin on their backs just like dolphins. This is an example of *convergent evolution*—when two distantly related

An enormous, lizardlike mososaur chases
an invertebrate ammonite through Mesozoic waters.

creatures come to look like each other because they live in a similar way.

But not all Mesozoic sea creatures were vertebrates! Then as now, most life forms were invertebrates, and there were many weird and distinctive kinds of spineless organisms swimming around in Mesozoic oceans.

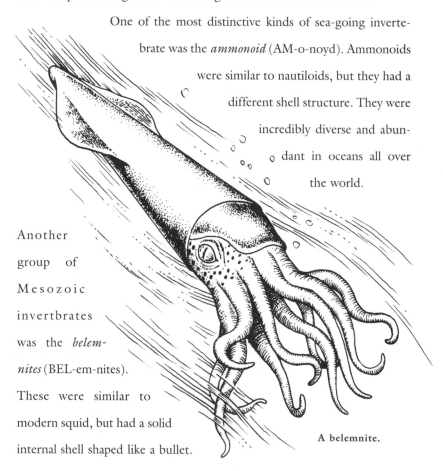

One of the most distinctive kinds of sea-going invertebrate was the *ammonoid* (AM-o-noyd). Ammonoids were similar to nautiloids, but they had a different shell structure. They were incredibly diverse and abundant in oceans all over the world.

Another group of Mesozoic invertbrates was the *belemnites* (BEL-em-nites). These were similar to modern squid, but had a solid internal shell shaped like a bullet.

A belemnite.

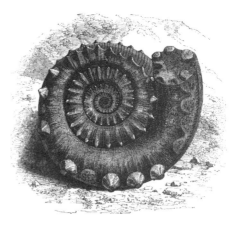

Drawings of ammonites
(above and bottom left)
and fossil ammonites
(bottom right).

This shape led early Native Americans to believe that belemnite fossils were petrified thunderbolts.

One very peculiar but very abundant group of Mesozoic sea creatures were the *rudist*s (ROO-dists). Rudists were clams that were shaped like corals, with one big cylinder-shaped shell and one small cap-shaped shell. Like corals today, rudists formed reefs and may have carried algae within their bodies so they could gather the sun's energy through photosynthesis, the way that plants create their own food.

Rudist fossils.

About 65 million years ago, life on Earth experienced yet another major crisis—another mass extinction—and the cast of characters changed again. The mass extinction that ended the Mesozoic Era was not as big as the one that ended the Paleozoic Era, but it's much more famous because it ended the age of the dinosaurs.

In the oceans, the biggest effects of this extinction were on invertebrates. At the end of the Mesozoic Era, the ammonoids, belemnites, rudists, and many other sea dwellers became extinct.

Perhaps the biggest loss was among the smallest organisms. Most of the *plankton*—food for almost all other organisms in the Mesozoic food chain—disappeared.

In all, about half of all the kinds of organisms in the world became extinct at the end of the Mesozoic Era, as many of the food chains that supported them were destroyed.

Scientists have argued for many years over what killed off the dinosaurs and other organisms at the end of the Mesozoic. Over the last 15 years, they've found evidence that a large object, such as a meteorite or comet, struck the earth around 65 million years ago, causing the extinctions. A large object hitting the earth would have thrown enormous quantities of dust and debris into the atmosphere, blocking out the sun and causing the death of plants that depended on it for survival. When the plants died, so did the animals that depended on the plants for food.

CENOZOIC LIFE IN THE OCEANS

The period from 65 million years ago to today is called the Cenozoic ("recent life") Era.

Following the mass extinction at the end of the Mesozoic, several million years passed before life recovered and new kinds of animals evolved to replace those that had disappeared.

As you can see when you go to the beach, Cenozoic oceans are dominated by clams, snails, crabs, starfish, sea urchins, bony fish, sharks, and whales. This is very different from sea life of the Paleozoic, with its brachiopods, trilobites, and crinoids; it's also somewhat different from sea life of the Mesozoic, with its ammonoids, rudists, and giant sea-going reptiles.

Sharks have been on earth for more than 300 million years, but they became very diverse and abundant in the Cenozoic Era. One of the most spectacular sea animals of the Cenozoic Era was the giant white shark, *Carcharodon megalodon* (car-CAR-o-don MEG-uh-lo-don), whose tooth is buried in the block of clay that comes with this kit.

Carcharodon megalodon is now extinct, but it was very similar to today's great white shark (the star of the movie *Jaws*). It was much larger than the great white, however, probably reaching lengths of 50 or even 60 feet. It lived between about 25 million years ago and about 3 million years ago, apparently only in the coastal waters of eastern North America. The giant white also had a giant appetite—its tooth marks on fossil bones tell us that it frequently ate whales!

No one knows why the giant white shark became extinct. It may have run out of food when many large whales disappeared from the western part of the Atlantic Ocean between 5 million and 3 million years ago.

LIFE IN THE OCEANS TODAY

The oceans are filled with more kinds of organisms today than ever before.

Coral reefs, located in places like Jamaica and Australia, are the homes for more kinds of living things than almost any other habitat on earth.

Hot springs in ocean floors, discovered by scientists in just the last 20 years, are home to very specialized types of animals, such as giant tube worms and white clams.

SHARKS!

Today, there are approximately 400 species of sharks swimming in the world's oceans. They play an important role in sea life. All sharks are predators, but only a few have been known to attack people.

A shark's skeleton is made mostly of cartilage, rather than bone. Because cartilage is less durable than bone, shark skeletons are rarely found as fossils.

Shark teeth—such as the ones buried in the clay block included with this kit—are very common fossils, though. Rocks from the Cenozoic Era are full of them! Sharks loose and replace their teeth throughout their lives, so a single shark can produce hundreds or even thousands of teeth.

If you go to the beach, you might find a fossil shark's tooth. You can tell a fossil shark's tooth because the fossil tooth is usually black or dark brown. Modern shark teeth are white.

Many kinds of fossil shark's teeth are known. The pictures below show the teeth of some common Cenozoic sharks.

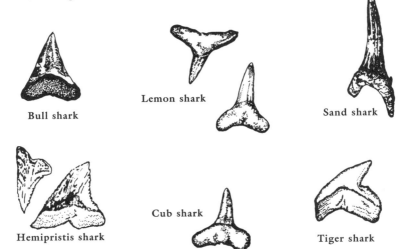

Bull shark

Lemon shark

Sand shark

Hemipristis shark

Cub shark

Tiger shark

Coastal wetlands and salt marshes—areas where the sea meets the land—are home to numerous types of animals. These animals live in the wetlands and marshes during one part of their lives and in the ocean during other parts.

Humans, who have existed for only about 3 million years, have begun to change the oceans, and not all of the changes are good for the life of the seas. Coral reefs today are being damaged by pollution, threatening the thousands of species that live there. Overfishing has decreased the catches at some of the world's best fishing grounds (such as the Grand Banks off New England) to such a degree that governments have told fishermen that they can no longer fish there for several years, in order to allow fish populations to rebuild. Although commercial whaling is no longer practiced by most countries, most kinds of whales remain very rare, and some may become extinct within the next 100 years.

The fossil record tells us that extinction is always followed by recovery, but it also tells us that recovery takes millions of years, and that once a type of animal or plant is extinct, it is gone forever and cannot be duplicated.

Carcharodon megalodon's jaws were big enough to hold these six men!

PART THREE

HOW DO WE KNOW ABOUT PREHISTORIC OCEANS?

How do we know all this about prehistoric oceans? After all, they were pre-historic. That means they existed before history—before there were people around to look at them and write down what they saw.

How can we know what happened in the past if no people were there to tell us? The answer lies in learning how to read the clues that are preserved in the Earth itself. It can be done, if you know what to look for.

READING THE ROCKS

The Earth's outer skin, or crust, is made of rocks. We classify rocks into three basic kinds, based on how they formed. Each kind of rock contains clues for reading history.

Igneous rocks are formed when melted rock, such as the lava in a volcano, cools and hardens. When lava cools, hard crystals begin to grow inside it.

Igneous rock.

If the lava cools quickly, the crystals don't have much time to grow, so they'll turn out small. If the lava cools slowly, the crystals have more time to grow and will be larger.

So we can recognize two kinds of igneous rocks, based on the size of the crystals they contain. Rocks with small crystals probably formed from lava that flowed out of a volcano and cooled quickly in the air. Rocks with very large crystals probably formed from lava that cooled deep within the earth.

Metamorphic rocks are formed when rocks are heated and squeezed deep in the Earth's crust. The heat and pressure change them into new, different rocks. You can often recognize metamorphic rocks because they contain streaks or swirls.

We know from laboratory experiments that different chemicals form in different conditions of heat and pressure. So if we find out what kinds of chemicals are in a metamorphic rock, we can sometimes determine how much the rock was squeezed or heated. This tells us something about the forces that were shaping

Metamorphic rock.

the Earth, and what conditions were like, at the time the rock was formed.

Sedimentary rocks form when other rocks are broken into tiny pieces by erosion and are deposited—usually by water—in layers of mud, sand, and gravel. These layers eventually harden and form new rocks. You can usually recognize sedimentary rocks because they are layered.

The size and shape of the little rock pieces in sedimentary rocks can tell us how far they traveled before they were deposited, or what conditions were like where

Sedimentary rock.

and when they were deposited. Small, round pieces, for example, have

CONTINENTAL DRIFT

If you look on a map at the eastern coast of South America and the western coast of Africa, you'll notice that they have some very strong similarities. They look a little bit like two pieces of a puzzle that would fit nicely together (if you could move them).

Scientists noticed these similarities many decades ago. They also noticed that similar fossils and rocks were found on the two continents.

How could the same life forms have developed on two continents that are separated by such a large ocean?

Discoveries and questions like these led to the theory of *continental drift*. This is the idea that the continents actually began as one large land mass that drifted apart over millions of years. The maps on page 43 show how scientists believe the Earth's continents have moved over time.

150 MILLION YEARS AGO

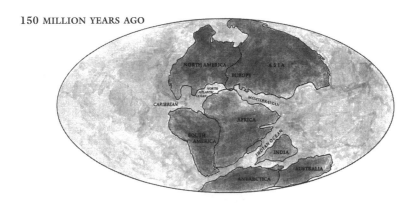

130 MILLION YEARS AGO

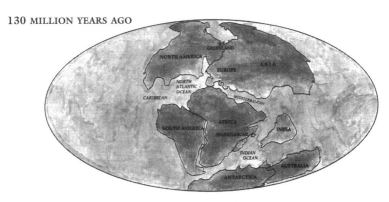

70 MILLION YEARS AGO

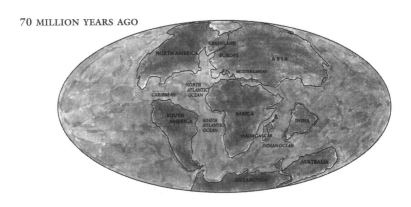

probably traveled farther than large, angular pieces, because they've been worn down and polished by the forces that moved them, such as wind and water.

There are some special types of sedimentary rocks that tell us about the history of the oceans:

Sometimes waves make ripples in the sand as they move over it. If this sand is buried quickly by more sand or mud, these ripple marks may be preserved. When the sand forms sandstone, a sedimentary rock, we can examine the ripples preserved in it and see what direction the waves were coming from millions of years ago.

Sea water is salty because chemicals, including salt, are eroded out of rocks and carried to the ocean by streams and rivers. Sometimes sea water collects in a shallow place near the edge of the ocean. There, it is heated by the sun until the water evaporates, leaving only the salt behind. If this happens again and again over millions of years, huge layers of salt may form. Many such layers have formed over the Earth's history, and today we mine rock salt from them. Wherever there is a salt mine today, you know there was once an ocean!

READING FOSSILS

Rocks are not alive and never were. But they can tell us about the history of life on Earth because sometimes the remains of living things become buried in mud or sand. After millions of years, the mud or sand turns into sedimentary rock, preserving the remains of the organism inside. These remains are called *fossils*.

Fossils are almost always the remains of the hard parts of organisms, such as shells or bones. This is because the soft flesh rots away very quickly or is eaten by other organisms. But sometimes organisms are buried very quickly, and traces of their soft parts are preserved, too. These are very exciting fossils to find. They give us a lot more information than we can get from just bones or shells.

READING HISTORY AT THE BEACH

Look at the sand at the beach, using a magnifying glass if you have one, and ask yourself: "Where did this sand come from?"

To answer this question, you must first ask other questions:

What kind of rocks did it used to be part of? (Hint: are there other rocks, perhaps in nearby mountains, that have crystals in them that look like these sand grains? If so, the sand may have come from those rocks.)

How did the rocks change into sand? (Hint: Watch the waves break on the shore. What are they doing to the sand grains? What would happen to a rock if you placed it in a fast-flowing stream or in the breaking waves?)

Are the sand grains rounded or angular? What does this tell you about their history? (Hint: sand from different areas of the same beach, or from different beaeches, may look different. If the sand grains are all very small and very round, they have probaly been traveling and worn down for a long time.)

What kind of rock would the sand form? (Hint: press some wet sand together in your hands. If this was a rock, what name would you give it?)

The fossil ripples preserved in this sandstone show that there was once a beach where the stone was found. Can you tell which direction the waves were moving?

How do we know that fossils were once alive, when we can't see them alive today? Scientists who study fossils are called *paleontologists*. They study fossils by comparing them to organisms living today. For example, some fossils resemble the bones of fish that live in the oceans today, so we believe that they were once the bones of ancient fish. Other fossils resemble the

TYPES OF FOSSILS

External brachiopod molds.

It's very difficult to become a fossil. After dying, most organisms decay or are eaten by scavengers or predators, so they can't become fossils. But if the remains of an organism are buried quickly in sand or mud, then a fossil may form.

Fossils are preserved in many ways. A *mold* is an impression of a shell or some other hard part in a rock, but the actual shell or hard part of the organism has been dissolved away.

A *cast* (sometimes called an *internal mold*) forms when sand or mud fills the inside of a shell and then hardens. If the shell itself disappears, all that is left is an impression of its inside.

Mineralization, or *petrification*, occurs when a shell or bone is buried in sand or mud. Water flowing through the ground carries dissolved minerals into the shell or bone and deposits them there. The original shell or bone usually dissolves away, leaving an almost exact copy made of stone.

Internal brachiopod molds.

shells of clams that live in the oceans today, so we believe that they were once the shells of living clams.

Most fossils are not exactly like any organism alive today. This is why we believe that some organisms that once lived on earth are no longer alive— they have become *extinct*. Some fossils closely resemble something alive today, but are slightly different. This is one reason we believe organisms change over time, from generation to generation—this process is called *evolution*. (When a life form changes over time, it is said to evolve.)

Just as the little grains inside a sedimentary rock can tell us about conditions when those grains were deposited, fossils can tell us about conditions when the organism was alive. For example, corals are animals that today live only in the ocean. They often build large colonial structures called *reefs* with their skeletons. So if you find a fossil coral inside a sedimentary rock, you know there was probably once an ocean in that spot, even if the nearest ocean today is hundreds or thousands of miles away.

Crinoid fossil.

HOW DO YOU FIND FOSSILS?

Fossils are usually found only in sedimentary rocks. Remains of organisms would be burned up in the lavas that make igneous rocks or destroyed by the heat and pressure that create metamorphic rocks. So if you want to look for fossils, first find some sedimentary rocks.

Of course, not all sedimentary rocks contain fossils—either because there was nothing alive in the area where the rocks formed, or because the remains of the organisms were destroyed before they could be preserved. But if there are fossils, you can usually find them by picking up flat pieces of rock and searching the surfaces carefully.

Look for shapes that resemble living things, or parts of living things.

The best places to look for fossils, of course, are usually those places where

Drawing of fossil
ichthyosaur skeleton.

fossils have been found before. Just because someone has visited a place and collected some fossils doesn't mean you can't find something new. Remember—every time you split open a rock and look inside, you're seeing things that no other human being has ever seen.

WHAT KIND OF ORGANISM IS THIS?

Once you find a shape that you think is a fossil, how do you know what it is, or was? How, for that matter, do you know it is a real fossil and not just a funny mark on a rock? The only way is to compare your find to something alive today, either by looking in museums, in books or other publications, or by comparing what is in the rock to an actual living thing in your hand.

Compare the shape, size, number of legs, eyes, shells, bones, grooves, spines, bumps, and any other features you can. Make a list of the similarities and differences. If it resembles no living organism, it doesn't mean it was never alive and is not a fossil. It might be (and indeed probably is) the remains of an extinct life form, one that is not alive anywhere on Earth today. But it could also be nothing more than a mark made by some non-living process, such as water flowing, or crystals or chemicals forming inside the rock.

If you decide that your find does resemble a living organism, then it probably is a fossil, belonging to the same group of organisms as the living one it resembles.

The next step is to name your fossil. It may be very similar or identical to one that scientists have studied and named before. If so, you would use the same name. But your fossil may be different from all other known fossils. It's possible that nothing exactly like it has ever been studied and named before. If so, you get to give it a new name.

To be certain your fossil is unique, you've got to look at as many other fossils as possible. Make sure that your fossil is distinctly different from fossils from other rock layers and other locations. You must read as much as possible about similar fossils, from this location and elsewhere. You should also go to museums to compare your fossil with others, and talk to paleontologists and other fossil collectors. Only then can you be sure that you have something no one has ever seen before.

If you believe your fossil is truly new, then you can give it a new name. Most scientific names of organisms are based on Latin or Greek, or on words from other languages with Latin or Greek endings. This is done to allow scientists around the world to understand each other, no matter what language they speak. You might name your fossil for the place it was found, for a distinctive feature of its body, or for the friend who helped you collect it.

For example, the fossil snail *Bulliopsis marylandica* is named for the state of Maryland, where it was found. The name *Nodonema granulatum* was given to a snail fossil found in Illinois. The name indicates that the shell is covered with nodes and granules. The fossil snail *Turritella*

Fossil cross-sections of crinoid stems.

mortoni, found in Alabama, was named for Samuel George Morton, a friend of the scientist who described it.

HOW OLD IS YOUR FOSSIL?

If someone asked you how old you are, you could give two kinds of answers. You might say you're younger than your parents, or older than one of your friends. These would be statements of your *relative age*—your age as compared to someone else's age. But you might also say that you are 12 years old. This would be a statement of your *numerical age*.

In just the same way, scientists who study the Earth can state the age of something in two different ways: relative and numerical. Relative ages are much easier. Using relative age is by far the most common way of dating rocks and the fossils found in them.

Relative dating of rocks depends on a simple principle called *superposition*. This principle says that unless the rocks have been disturbed—by an earthquake, for example—the oldest layers are found on the bottom and the youngest layers on the top. This makes sense if we think about how sedimentary rocks form: layers of mud, sand, and gravel are deposited one on top of the other. A younger layer cannot normally be slipped in underneath an older one.

If you look at a stack of rocks (in a river bank, quarry, or roadcut, for example), you'll notice different fossils are found in different layers. The principle of superposition tells us that the fossils in the lower layers are older than the fossils in the upper layers. Because we've observed that distinct fossils are found in each layer of rock, different types of fossils can be markers for different time periods.

With this understanding, we can travel far and wide examining the order in which different fossils occur in different rock layers. Eventually, we can learn to predict what layer is indicated by what fossil. Layers can thus be dated by their fossils.

Because it is difficult to remember long lists of fossils, scientists have grouped fossils that occur in the same layers together and given these groups names. These names have then been combined into a *Geological Time Scale*. This is the system of names and dates used by all geologists and paleontologists to tell time in the rocks of the Earth. (See page 13.)

Numerical dating is more complicated than relative dating, because it requires special equipment, but the principle is also very simple. Crystals in igneous rocks may contain a radioactive element that changes into a different element at a very regular rate over time. We can measure this rate in a laboratory, along with how much of the element has changed. From these measurements we can calculate the age of the igneous rock.

Numerical dates usually come from crystals in igneous rocks, not from fossils themselves; relative dates come from the fossils found in sedimentary rocks. So to connect numerical dates to relative ones, you need to find places where igneous and sedimentary rocks are close to each other.

So when you find a fossil, how do you know how old it is? Fortunately, a lot of the work has already been done for you. You first identify the fossil. You then find out (usually by going to the library) in what layers and with what other fossils it has been found before. Using the Geological Time Scale, you can assign an age to the layer in which you found your fossil. Because each grouping of fossils in the Time Scale has been assigned a numerical age, you can use this numerical age for your fossil.

THE SEARCH CONTINUES

The most important thing to remember about science is that it never ends. There is no end to the number of questions that can be asked, and there are always new ideas to be investigated.

No conclusion is ever final. Every scientific statement can be overturned if enough evidence turns up that does not agree with it. New discoveries are made all the time, and new interpretations are always being made about old discoveries.

You might make important discoveries about the history of the oceans and their life—discoveries that will change our ideas about the past. All you have to do is never stop looking, questioning, and learning.

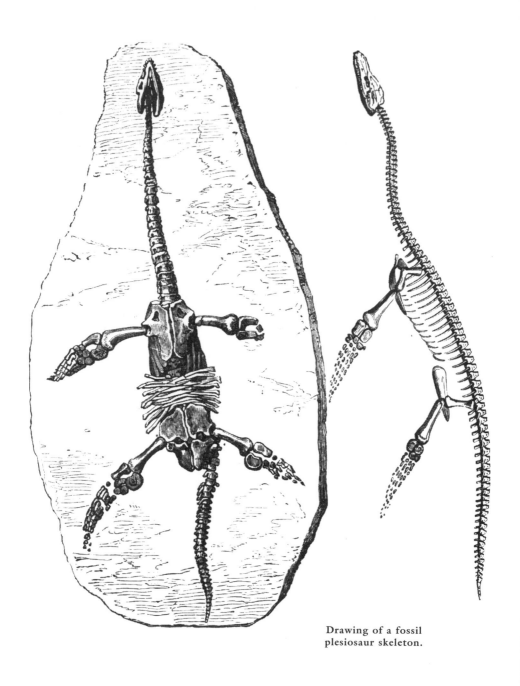

Drawing of a fossil
plesiosaur skeleton.

PART FOUR

WHERE DO PEOPLE STUDY FOSSILS?

Our knowledge about life in prehistoric oceans has come from studies of fossils. Those fossils are mostly stored in museums. You may be used to thinking about museums only for the large objects—like dinosaur skeletons—that they put on public display. But behind the scenes, museums hold much more.

Museums are like libraries for rocks and fossils. Just like books in libraries, the rocks and fossils in museum collections are used as sources of information for scientists who study the history of the Earth and its life.

Museum collections (or books and other publications based on museum collections) can help fossil hunters and collectors answer important questions: Is your fossil new, or has it been described before? Is it an extinct organism, or one that is still alive today? What other organisms are most closely related to your fossil? What is your fossil's relative age?

Building and preserving museum collections helps scientists, students, and others continue to answer these kinds of questions, giving us a clearer and clearer picture of the Earth's prehistoric past.

One of the world's oldest known fossils,
this 3.5 billion–year–old stromatolite—formed
from layers of algae—was found in Australia.

PART FIVE

EXCAVATE YOUR OWN SHARKS' TEETH

Now you're ready to excavate, restore, and identify fossils, just as paleontologists do.

Inside this kit are two sharks' teeth buried in a slab of soft clay. One is a full-size replica of a tooth from *Carcharodon megalodon*, a 25-million-year-old ancestor of the Great White Shark. The other is a real fossil tooth from a shark that lived about 16 million years ago. You'll find both teeth in the same slab of clay. The replica tooth is much larger, and is embedded in a slab of rock that you can use as a base for displaying it. Get ready to excavate!

MATERIALS INCLUDED IN THIS KIT:

- A rectangular slab of claylike sedimentary rock that holds the sharks' teeth

- Wooden excavation tool

- Black paint disk and a paintbrush for restoring the replica tooth

OTHER MATERIALS YOU'LL NEED:

- Newspaper or plastic bag to cover your work surface

- Water

- Bucket or basin in which to soak the slab of rock

- Soft brush (a paintbrush or an old toothbrush)

- Tissue paper or paper towels

- White glue (Elmer's Glue-All, for example)

- Clear wax or shoe polish

THE EXCAVATION

First you'll need to excavate your sharks' teeth from the slab of clay. Take your time and do it carefully. Make sure to cover your work area with newspaper or plastic, because this can be messy work! Look carefully as you dig—the real fossil tooth is small and may be hidden inside a chip of clay. Follow these steps:

1. Fill your bucket or a basin with enough water to cover the slab of sedimentary rock. Remove the slab from the plastic and place it in the water. Let it soak for a few minutes, until it gets soft. Save the water in case the clay gets hard and you need to soak it again.

2. Place the slab on a large piece of paper and dry its surface with tissue paper. Using the wooden tool, carefully dig through the clay one layer at a time. Continue your excavation until you discover both the smaller

fossil tooth and the replica on its base plate. (Don't worry if the base plate is broken—you can glue it back together later.) Keep digging until both teeth are removed from the soft brown sediment. Both specimens are harder than the sedimentary rock, so your wooden tool won't damage them.

CLEANING AND RESTORING THE TEETH

1. Rinse the teeth under running water, gently scrubbing off the clay with a paintbrush or an old toothbrush. Make sure you get all the dirt off the teeth. Then dry them with soft tissue paper.

2. With a paintbrush, apply a clear wax to the small, natural shark's tooth. Let it dry, then polish it with a soft cloth.

3. Before you can restore the giant replica tooth, you must make sure its base plate is completely dry. You can leave the tooth in a warm room for two days, or you can put it in the oven at low heat (100–120°F) until it is dry. Be careful—too much heat could make it crack.

4. Once the replica and base plate are dry, you'll paint the tooth to make it look the way it did in the mouth of *Carcharodon megalodon*. The paint disk in this kit works like the paint in a set of watercolors. Dip the paintbrush in water and dab it on the paint disk until some of the paint smears on the brush. Paint the tooth to look like the one pictured on the package cover of this kit. You'll see that the area in the center is a

darker shade of black than the rest of the tooth. Try to match the variations in shading as you paint.

5. If the base plate is broken into several pieces, glue it together with white glue. Then apply a clear wax or shoe polish to the tooth and the plate. Let it dry, and polish it with a soft cloth.

IDENTIFYING THE FOSSIL TOOTH

You already know that the larger tooth is about 25 million years old and comes from Carcharodon megalodon (see page 36). The other tooth you excavated is about 16 million years old, but you'll need to study it in order to identify the kind of shark it belonged to.

Examine the fossil tooth and make some notes about its main features. Is it long or short? Does it have jagged or smooth edges? How big is it? Draw a sketch of the tooth. Now compare this information to the drawings on page 37, and see if you can identify what kind of shark the tooth came from.

Fossil tooth of
Carcharodon megalodon.

Congratulations! Your excavation is complete. Now you can label your sharks' teeth and display them as the first two specimens in your fossil collection. Someday they might help you identify other finds!

WANT TO LEARN MORE?

If you'd like to learn more about fossils and paleontology, you can write to the author of this book and receive information on educational programs and membership in the Paleontological Research Institution. Be sure to send along your name, address, and age. Write to:

Dr. Warren Allmon, Director
Paleontological Research Institution
1259 Trumansburg Road
Ithaca, New York 14850–1398

ABOUT THE AUTHOR

Warren Allmon earned his Ph.D. from Harvard University's Department of Earth and Planetary Sciences, where he specialized in studies of the evolution of fossil and recent mollusks. He is the author of numerous scholarly works on paleontology and has taught geology and biology at the University of South Florida. Since 1992, he has been Director of the Paleontological Research Institution in Ithaca, New York. With more than 1.5 million specimens, the institution is home to one of the ten largest collections of fossil invertebrates in America.